GO
DIEGO
GO!

ANIMAL RESCUER

Physical

Published by Scholastic Inc., 90 Old Sherman Turnpike, Danbury, CT 06816

SCHOLASTIC and associated logos are trademarks and/or registered trademarks of Scholastic Inc.

ISBN 0-439-90703-9

Printed in the U.S.A.

First Scholastic Printing, December 2006

Diego
Saves the Tapir

by
Christine Ricci

illustrated by
Art Mawhinney

SCHOLASTIC INC.

New York Toronto London Auckland Sydney
Mexico City New Delhi Hong Kong Buenos Aires

"I love camping," Diego exclaimed as he and Baby Jaguar set up their tent. Just then, they heard a splashing sound coming from the lake, followed by footsteps. Then, a large animal stuck its head into the tent.

It was Mommy Mountain Tapir!

"Diego, I need your help!" she cried. "It's getting dark and my little tapir isn't home yet."

"Don't worry," said Diego. "We can use my special camera, Click, to find your baby."

Click zoomed through the forest and located
the little tapir.

"Look!" exclaimed Baby Jaguar. "Little Tapir is lost.
And there's a puma nearby!"

"Tapirs are afraid of pumas. We've got to find him!"
said Diego. "*¡Al rescate!* To the rescue!"

"We've got to get to Little Tapir fast. Run! Run!
¡Corre! ¡Corre!" urged Diego as he and Baby Jaguar ran
down the path.

But the path ended at a large river filled with rapids.
Diego and Baby Jaguar skidded to a stop.

"Diego, we're going to need something to ride across this river," said Baby Jaguar.

"My Rescue Pack can transform into anything we need. *¡Actívate!*" shouted Diego.

Rescue Pack quickly transformed into a raft.

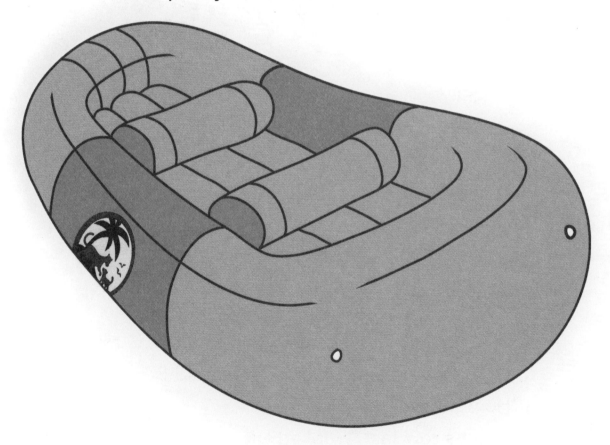

Diego and Baby Jaguar jumped into the raft.

"The water is moving so fast," said Baby Jaguar.
"How will we get across?"

"Let's row fast," replied Diego. "Row, row, row!
¡Rema, rema, rema!"

"Great rowing!" exclaimed Diego as he and
Baby Jaguar landed on the other side of the river.

13

As they climbed out of the raft, Diego and Baby Jaguar heard giggling. "Bobos!" It was the Bobo Brothers. They were shaking a tree to get the fruit to fall down. But the shaking was causing some branches to break!

"We have to stop the Bobo Brothers! Freeze, Bobos!" shouted Diego.

The Bobo Brothers froze. Then they called, "Oops! Sorry!" and scampered off.

"Uh-oh, Diego!" gasped Baby Jaguar.

Diego looked up and saw a little pygmy marmoset hanging onto a loose tree branch.

"He's falling!" cried Baby Jaguar.

"We have to catch the pygmy marmoset! Reach out and catch him! *¡Agárralo!*" Diego reached up and caught the pygmy marmoset just in time.

Diego helped the pygmy marmoset to a safe branch.
Then he and Baby Jaguar ran on until they came to a fork
in the road. "Which way should we go, Diego?" wondered
Baby Jaguar.

"We need an animal that can fly and see which path
leads to the little tapir," said Diego. "Let's use my spotting
scope to find an animal that flies!"

18

Through his spotting scope, Diego saw lots of animals, but he only saw one that could fly. "The Blue Morpho Butterfly can help us!" he exclaimed.

"To tell the Blue Morpho Butterfly to fly, we have to flap our arms like butterfly wings," said Diego.

"Fly! *¡Vuela!*" called Diego and Baby Jaguar as they flapped their arms up and down. The butterfly soared high into the sky.

The Blue Morpho Butterfly spotted the little mountain tapir and called down to Diego. "Take the stone path to get to the little tapir. And hurry! A puma is nearby!"

"*¡Gracias!*" called Diego and Baby Jaguar.

As they ran down the stone path, Diego called out,
"Hide from the puma, Little Tapir! Hide! *¡Esconde!*"
Little Tapir heard their warning and quickly found a
safe hiding spot.

Little Tapir hid so well that the puma walked right by him!

When Diego and Baby Jaguar arrived at the tall
grass, they didn't see Little Tapir, either.
"Little Tapir, where are you?" called Diego.

Suddenly they heard a small squeaky voice coming from the tall grass. "I'm over here!"

Diego ran over to the grass and gently lifted Little Tapir out of his hiding spot. "You're safe now," Diego said, as he gave Little Tapir a big hug. "Let's get you home."

When they arrived back at the campsite, Mommy Mountain Tapir was so happy to see her baby. The little tapir and his mommy curled up next to the tent where Diego and Baby Jaguar were snuggling down for the night.

"*¡Misión cumplida!* Rescue complete!"whispered Diego. "That was a great animal adventure!"

Nick Jr. Play-to-Learn™ Fundamentals
Skills every child needs, in stories every child will love!

 colors + shapes
Recognizing and identifying basic shapes and colors in the context of a story.

 emotions
Learning to identify and understand a wide range of emotions: happy, sad, excited, frustrated, etc.

 imagination
Fostering creative thinking skills through role-play and make-believe.

 math
Recognizing early math in the world around us: patterns, shapes, numbers, sequences.

 music + movement
Celebrating the sounds and rhythms of music and dance.

 physical
Building coordination and confidence through physical activity and play.

 problem solving
Using critical thinking skills (observing, listening, following directions) to make predictions and solve problems.

 reading + language
Developing a lifelong love of reading through high interest stories and characters.

 science
Fostering curiosity and an interest in the natural world around us.

 social skills + cultural diversity
Developing respect for others as unique, interesting people.

Physical

Conversation Spark

Questions and activities for play-to-learn parenting.

Tapirs (TAY-pers) are animals that live in the rainforest. What other animals can you name? Where do those animals live? Can you name some animals that live near you?

For more parent and kid-friendly activities, go to www.nickjr.com.

ENGLISH/SPANISH GLOSSARY
and PRONUNCIATION GUIDE

ENGLISH	SPANISH	PRONUNCIATION
To the rescue	Al rescate	al res-CAH-teh
Run	Corre	KOH-ray
Activate	Actívate	ahk-TEE-vah-tay
Row	Rema	REH-mah
Catch him	Agárralo	ah-GAH-rah-loh
Fly	Vuela	voo-EH-lah
Thank you	Gracias	GRAH-see-ahs
Hide	Escóndete	es-KOHN-deh-tay
Rescue	Misión	mee-see-OHN
Complete	Cumplida	coom-PLEE-dah